Hmm . . . another ending?

Reading time won't always be quiet time! Children will often interrupt with questions and comments that will help them understand the story, such as "*Why does Mrs Wolf decide not to eat Funny Feet?*" Encourage your child to tell you what he thinks will happen or to tell the story with a different ending.

Picture talk

Encourage your child to look at the pictures carefully. Ask questions such as *"Why do you think Mrs Wolf called the duckling Funny Feet?"* and *"What do you think Funny Feet would like to eat for lunch?"* Looking at the pictures can help budding readers look for clues and predict what comes next in the story.

Have a good time and enjoy the magic of the story!

Wendy Cooling

Wendy Cooling
Reading Consultant

For my brother Sam, with love – SR

LONDON, NEW YORK, SYDNEY, DELHI, PARIS,
MUNICH and JOHANNESBURG

First published in Great Britain in 2000
by Dorling Kindersley Limited,
9 Henrietta Street, London WC2E 8PS

2 4 6 8 10 9 7 5 3 1

A CIP catalogue record for this book is available from the British Library.

ISBN 0-7513-7243-9

Colour reproduction by Dot Gradations, UK

Printed in Hong Kong by Wing King Tong

Acknowledgements:
Series Reading Consultant: Wendy Cooling **Series Activities Advisor:** Lianna Hodson
Photographer: Steve Gorton **Models:** Crispin and Jemima Dunne; Shayan Talabany

ANE FOR A'

Fun Ideas for the Storyteller

Not Now, Mrs Wolf is a delightfully funny story with lively, playful language that is ideal for reading aloud. Children will love looking at the funny pictures and anticipating the surprise ending. Be prepared to read this story again and again!

Read on to find out how to get the most fun out of this story.

Join in and make believe

Add excitement to your reading by joining in with the actions of the characters: tickle your child's toes when Mrs Wolf tickles Funny Feet; count the woolly clouds in the picture; give a kiss on the nose and then pretend to sleep for a moment. Children will love this game of make-believe.

Share the reading

Let your child do as much as possible – turn the pages, join in with words, and point things out in the pictures. As the story becomes familiar, your child will want to do more of the reading. Help if he gets stuck and don't worry about mistakes. It's your child's enthusiasm that matters most.

Not Now, Mrs Wolf!

Shen Roddie

Selina Young

A Dorling Kindersley Book

Mrs Wolf was starving.

"I could eat a big, fat duck!" she said.

And just as she said that, she found an egg.

A large, pale blue duck's egg.

"Hmmm . . . I could eat you. But not now," said Mrs Wolf. "I'll let you hatch, first. Then I'll have a nice, tender duckling for my supper."

Mrs Wolf took the egg home and sat on it gently. "Hurry up, dear!" she said. And just as she said that, out stumbled a wet little duckling.

"Mama!" quacked the duckling.

Mrs Wolf jumped. "Mama? Where's your mama?" she asked, smacking her lips. "I'll bet your mama's twice as nice. She'd make a better supper than you!" thought Mrs Wolf.

But the duckling snuggled up closer.
"Ugh, you're too wet for my
supper," muttered Mrs Wolf.

“Mama! Mama!”
quacked the duckling.
“I’m not your mama,
you silly little Funny Feet,”
said Mrs Wolf.

Mrs Wolf licked Funny Feet dry.
She licked his head, his arms,
his legs, his tummy.
Funny Feet giggled.
"There, silly wiggles!"
said Mrs Wolf. "You're
nice and sweet, and dry
as a biscuit!"

She ruffled his feathers.
Then she sat him
on the table. She
was very hungry.
"Hmmm . . . you fluffy
little treat!" she
thought. "I could eat
you. But not now. If
I let you grow a little,
there'll be more of
you to eat."

Hmmmmm
Plum Sauce

So Mrs Wolf looked up a book on ***'How to Grow Fat Ducks'***. It said: Eat, Play and Sleep.
"Easy!" said Mrs Wolf.

For days, Mrs Wolf stood by her hot stove. She tossed pancakes, cooked chocolate muffins, jam tarts, and jibbly jellies. Funny Feet ate and ate and ate.

When he had a tummy ache, Mrs Wolf rubbed it better. She gave his tummy a little squeeze.

"My, my, honeypot! You ***are*** getting fat!" she said. "I could eat you. But not now," she thought.

"Now we must play. Happy ducklings make fat ducks!" said Mrs Wolf. She took Funny Feet to the park. They danced round the tree trunk.

They played hide-and-seek, and when Funny Feet fell over, Mrs Wolf kissed his knee all better. "There, there! Who's a brave little sugar bun then!" she said, giving him a cuddle.

"Come along, pom pom, let's play some more," said Mrs Wolf. She pushed Funny Feet on the swings and gave him a piggyback ride. "Hang on tight, my little yo-yo!" she called.

Then it was time for lunch. Mrs Wolf spread out the blanket. She opened up the picnic basket and pulled out her last sandwich.

She looked at it long and hard. Then she gave it to Funny Feet. "Here, my little sugar puff!" she said. "You must get nice and plump."

After lunch, Mrs Wolf took Funny Feet out into the meadow for a nap.

She flopped on the grass. Funny Feet plopped on her tummy.

Mrs Wolf tickled his toes.
Funny Feet giggled.
They counted woolly
cloud sheep.

Then Mrs Wolf sang a soft wolf lullaby.
She kissed Funny Feet's nose.
Soon they both fell fast
asleep in the sunshine.

When they got home, Mrs Wolf's tummy grumbled and drumbled. She was very, very hungry.

She gazed at Funny Feet for a long, long time.
Finally she opened her larder. It was empty!
“Oh dear . . .” sighed Mrs Wolf.
Slowly, she went to turn the oven on.

"What's for dinner, Mama?" asked Funny Feet.
"Guess!" said Mrs Wolf.
"A plum?" asked Funny Feet.
"No, bigger," said Mrs Wolf, as she crept slowly towards Funny Feet.

"A potato?" asked Funny Feet.
"No, fatter and juicier," said Mrs Wolf, reaching for Funny Feet.

“I know!” cried Funny Feet,
and he dashed out of the kitchen door.

"Is *this* our dinner?" asked Funny Feet, as he pushed a huge watermelon through the door. Mrs Wolf looked at Funny Feet, all big and fat and happy.

Then she looked at the
watermelon, all big and
fat and juicy.

"Why," laughed Mrs Wolf,
"of course it is!
This is our dinner and
we shall eat it. Now!"

And slosh, slosh, spit, spit, they did!

Slosh

Activities to Enjoy

If you've enjoyed this story, you might like to try some of these simple, fun activities with your child.

Have your own picnic

Carry on the fun of the story by having your own picnic – pretend or real. Decide who you'll invite – real guests, characters from the story, or favourite toys. Imagine what the guests might like to eat if they could have anything in the world. This will encourage your child to use her imagination and is lots of fun, too!

Making the food

Make pretend food . . . or the real thing. Use play dough or draw and colour pictures on card and then cut them out. Or just use plastic toy food. Children will also enjoy helping you make healthy picnic foods, such as sandwiches and fruit salad.

Preparing for the picnic

Show your child how to set places around a cloth. Encourage him to set a plate and a cup for each guest. Count as you do this. This gives your child a chance to practise counting and helps him work out that four guests mean four plates and four cups will be needed.

To make simple place cards, fold a piece of card in half and ask your child to draw a picture on it. Help write each guest's name. Can your child write his own name? Don't worry if this is only a scribble! Now help your child match each guest's place card with his place at the picnic.

Enjoy your picnic!

Join in with the picnic and chat to the guests. Plan some games, too – perhaps play hide-and-seek like Mrs Wolf and Funny Feet do at the park. Imagine what Funny Feet and Mrs Wolf might do after they eat *their* watermelon!

Other Share-a-Story titles to collect:

The Caterpillar That Roared
by Michael Lawrence
illustrated by Alison Bartlett

Nigel's Numberless World
by Lucy Coats
illustrated by Neal Layton

Are You Spring?
by Caroline Pitcher
illustrated by Cliff Wright